Consume Me

A Stalker Possessive Billionaire Romance

Billionaire Boy's Club

Book 3

KeKe Renée

Latest Releases By Keke Renée:

- Wet Heat (Wet Heat Series Book 1)
- Everytime We Touch Novelette (Wet Heat Book 2 Series)
- His Peace, Her Pleasure
- Baby, It's Cold Outside
- Love Don't Live Here Anymore, Vanessa Andrew Book 1
- Love Don't Live Here Anymore, Isabella Andrew Book2
- One Night Only-A Novelette (Love By Design Book 1)
- Cassian and Savannah (Love By Design Book 2)
- Deidra's Love (Love By Design Book 3)
- Protecting Bria (Special Force Operation Alphas)
- Sensual: A Brother's Best Friend Romance
- Seek To Please Book 1
- Seek To Touch Book 2
- Seek To Bare Book 3
- Seek To Love Book 4

• Protecting Chanel (Special Forces Operation Alphas)
  • Seek To Trust Book 5
  • Seek To Earn Book 6
  • Tease Me Book 1
  • Please Me Book 2
  • Consume Me Book 3

I WANT TO THANK FIRST the readers for loving these characters so much and waiting so long for them to come back.

Disclaimer

THIS WORK OF FICTION contains strong language and explicit sexual content and is only intended for mature readers. This story may contain unconventional situations, language, and sexual encounters that may offend some readers. This book is for mature readers (18+).

Introduction

Are you signed up for my newsletter?

Join today and find out all the latest in new releases, contests, giveaways, sneak peeks and more.

https://BookHip.com/BKRPJL

Synopsis

Being stalked and claimed by a billionaire, wasn't on Emersyn's agenda.

Emerson Randolph works a regular job at a regular bookstore. Shy and curvy, Emerson has come to accept that romance isn't on the cards for her. The most exciting thing in her life is losing herself in romance novels and fantasizing about one day being swept off her feet.

Being stalked wasn't part of her fantasy.

Until her stalker reveals himself as Esteban Munoz, billionaire extraordinaire. This handsome playboy has the world at his feet and anything within his reach, and now he wants Emerson.

Will Esteban bring Emerson's fantasies to life, or will she shy away from the most exciting thing that's ever happened to her.

Go ahead, indulge in Book three from the Billionaire Boys Club. These interconnected standalone romances will bring your fantasies to life.

Chapter 1

Emersyn

I tried my best to balance the bag of groceries in my hand and the phone in the other. After leaving my book club tonight, I was ready to crack open the latest novel we'd picked up.

"Are you home yet?" Sanya asked.

Leaning down I stumbled to pick up the keys on the ground, when a large hand reached out, snatched them up, and held them out to me. Rising straight up, I stared into the sexiest, darkest coal black eyes I'd ever seen before.

"Do you need some help?" he asked. His deep gravelly voice pierced my heart.

"Ye-Yes," I stammered, clearing my throat. He extended his hand holding the keys. He grazed my fingers. With deliberate intent to not stare, I took the keys back.

"Emersyn, are you okay?!" Sanya yelled.

I nodded like she was here in front of me, instead of on the phone to answer her question. I felt like I was in a trance gazing at the man in front of me smoking a cigar. Smirking at me, he took the phone out of my hand without protest and spoke to Sanya.

He angled a glance down at me. "Emersyn looks fine to me," he said into my phone.

I finally blinked, my eyes coming out of the weird spell he had on me and glared at him. "That's my phone!" I snapped, rolling my neck and poking my lip out.

I tried to grab the phone out of his hand.

"Who is this?" Sanya barked.

Licking his lips, the stranger closed the space between us. "Tell her you're okay, Emersyn."

Why I would consider going along with his command left me confused. But in the next breath I found myself following his order. "Sanya, I'm fine." I hung up the phone and turned on my heel to walk up the stairs of my apartment when he stepped in front of me again.

His large, calloused hand stretched out to me. "I'm Esteban Munoz."

Glancing down at his offered hand, I shook it, feeling his tight grip. I pulled away to avoid his intense stare and lowered my eyes.

My skin became erect with goosebumps. "Emersyn Randolph," I murmured. Meanwhile I was cursing in my head for giving him my real name.

He cocked his head to the side. "Nice to meet you, Emersyn."

Sliding the key in the door, I looked over my shoulder as he stood at the bottom of the stairs. I stepped inside my apartment and shut the door behind me. I immediately headed to the window, moved the curtain aside, and watched Esteban slide inside a long stretch limo I never noticed.

"Esteban," I whispered, easing my jacket off and stepping out of my high heels. I'm exhausted from this long day. After the book club meeting, I told Sanya I would have lunch with her tomorrow after she gets off work at the bar. I put my groceries away then poured a glass of wine, thinking about the man that I ran into who held me hostage with his beautiful stare. His intensity gave me chills all over again.

The last date I had was three months ago and the guy only wanted to come back to my place and have sex. I pretty much put myself on a timeout with dating men because they all turn out the same as my ex-boyfriend, Dwayne. We were college sweethearts, and I thought we were headed for marriage one day, but I got the shock of my life when a woman showed up at my college dorm room pregnant. Now three years later, I see them happy and in love on social media.

Living in New York and working as a cashier at a bookstore was my dream. All of my life I wanted to be surrounded by books and meet my favorite authors. Being single in the city, I lived through all of the romance novels' characters, hoping I'd one day run into the man of my dreams and fall in love.

"Wishful thinking, Emersyn." I snickered, gulping the rest of my wine. Undoing my ponytail, I let my braids fall down to my back, turning the channel on the tv to the local news and pausing at what was being shown.

"We have the opening of the nightclub *Passions* in one month and the billionaire bachelor and owner, Esteban Munoz, is letting women come in free for the first weekend. Wonder who will be on his arm?" the Channel Seven News anchor reported. I froze, staring at the same face I met a little less than an hour ago.

"Esteban Munoz, billionaire bachelor," I muttered, reaching for my phone, then dialing Sanya's number.

"Emersyn, this better be good." Sanya's groggy voice seeped through the phone.

"Sanya, you won't believe what happened to me."

I heard her yawning through the phone. "What happened?"

"The guy that picked up my keys from the ground? I saw him on tv."

"Huh."

I hugged myself, the excitement building in my chest. "He's a billionaire!"

"Oookay." She hesitated, like I'd lost my mind. She's used to being surrounded by money with Gerald.

My feet began to move because I could not contain my nervous energy. I swallowed the sudden lump in my throat. "Okay. Sanya, why is he in the Bronx in the middle of the night?"

"Emersyn, calm down."

She must have known I was up pacing. "I'm calm," I said in a breathy voice.

"Are you pacing right now?"

I stopped in the middle of the room. I looked around the room as if she had cameras in my place. "Umm. No."

She chuckled. "Girl, I know you. Anyway, he's in the Bronx. So? It doesn't mean anything."

"The news said he's opening a club and having women come in free for the first night. What if he's some crazy lunatic searching for women?"

"Emersyn, how much have you drunk tonight?"

I glanced down at the empty bottle of wine I had finished off. "A glass or two."

"Sounds like you are reading too much into that book we discussed tonight."

"You are the last person to call me out. How many times did you think Gerald was full of shit."

Sanya giggled on the other end of the call. "Get some sleep and we can talk about it tomorrow at lunch."

"Fine, tell Gerald I said good luck."

"Sassy, aren't we?" Sanya titters, ending the call.

"Sassy, my ass. There's a reason he's out here past midnight, probably looking for a one-night stand."

* * *

The next morning after barely sleeping, I started my day by eating a large breakfast, showering, and going into the bookstore early to get started on inventory. My boss, Louise, came around the corner carrying a stack of books by my favorite author, Delaney Diamond. Seeing the number of indie authors in the store, on top of book events when they came for signings, plus getting to take pictures and signed autographs was why I loved working here.

Louise sat the books to the side, walked around the counter, and logged into the cash register. "This is the last stack of books for the window display."

"Thanks, I can get them up in a minute." I removed the trash off the counter and placed the empty boxes in the corner. Louise's store front was in the heart of the Bronx with good foot traffic near a coffee shop and a few restaurants. I was one of her first employees when she opened this place three years ago.

"How was your night?" Louise asked as she unlocked the front door and put the open sign out.

"Nothing much besides tv, wine, and a good book." I grinned.

Louise gave me a look and shook her head. "No dates?"

"Nope. Men aren't checking for me and I for sure ain't looking for them."

She rolled her eyes at me. Louise being married with two kids, and a few years older than me at thirty-four to my thirty, she always preached about letting things happen naturally.

"Emersyn, all you do is think negatively or think every guy is going to be like the books you read." Louise helped put up a romance book by author L.K. Ryan.

"Oh, I haven't read that one yet. *Vincenzo*," I said.

Louise snatched the book out of my hands. "Focus because the same way you fantasize about meeting Prince Charming is the same for men expecting the perfect woman."

"I don't expect Prince Charming."

She fluttered her lashes. "Could have fooled me."

"What's that supposed to mean?"

We both turned our heads at the door chimes and my breath caught at the person walking inside. Then my eyes narrowed into slits.

"Hello, welcome to *Books R Us*. Is there anything we can help you with?" Louise spoke to Esteban, but his eyes were trained on me for some reason.

"She can help me," Esteban responded, sliding his tongue across his lips.

Louise looked from Esteban to me, and her lips curled up into a smile. "Emersyn is one of my best employees. I am sure she can help you with anything."

I whipped my head around. "I-I-I'm actually slammed with stocking the shelves," I stuttered, feeling my body heat up and my hands get sweaty. There was something about this man that felt like he'd be the best and the worst thing for me.

"I can handle the shelves, Emersyn. Go ahead and help Mister... I forgot to get your name?" Louise demanded, and I wanted to curse her out for putting me on blast.

"Esteban Munoz." Our eye contact never dropped. Just his presence alone spoke volumes and I hated how my body reacted.

"Esteban, Emersyn would love to assist you." Louise's giggling brought me out of the trance I was under.

I blew out a long breath and asked, "Anything specific you wanted to look at?" Whirling around the counter, I moved closer to him with my arms folded over my chest.

Esteban smirked at me. "Bondage."

My eyes ballooned wide at his response. "I'm sorry what did you say?"

"You heard me."

"Bondage," I repeated, my breathing labored.

He moved to close the distance between us. "Bondage, books on learning rope play."

I nodded in understanding. I knew he was fucking with me, but I went along with his games and went to the erotica section in the store and grabbed a few things.

"Anything else?"

"Your phone number."

"No."

Esteban traced a finger down my cheek, and I felt my breath catch in my chest. "I've never been told no before."

I gave him a smile. "First time for everything. Will that be cash or credit?"

Grimacing, he reached in his pocket, pulled a stack of money out, and handed it over.

"Cash and keep the change."

"That's a hundred dollars!" I exclaimed.

He shrugged his shoulders. "I like the customer service and want to tip."

Bagging up his books, I ignored his statement and passed over the receipt. "Here you are, Mr. Munoz and thank you for shopping at *Books R Us*."

His eyes changed focus from my face to my body, and he covered my hand on top of the counter. "I want to take you out."

"No."

"Again, a no word." He leaned against the glass counter.

"Anything else you would like to buy?"

"You."

I laughed right in his face and shook my head at him. "I won't be one of your paid off women."

The wide grin spread across his face, and it sent that same excitement through me I had last night at his longing look of lust.

Reaching in his pocket, he pulled out a business card. "My club is opening in a month. I'd love to see you there and bring a friend." Esteban didn't wait for an answer. He simply grabbed the books off the counter and left. I flipped the card over and back to the front. "Esteban Munoz, CEO and Owner of Munoz industries," I muttered.

The feeling of emptiness left behind was startling, like I wanted the chase and needed his focus to be on me.

A man I barely knew and only met for a brief second held a lot of space in my mind and surprisingly, my heart. Finishing off the task of restocking the shelves, I put Esteban Munoz out of my mind and completed the rest of my shift.

Chapter 2

Esteban

The typical day for me was fielding calls and meetings about my businesses around the world. My father built a company that handled everything from the tech industry to nightlife. I couldn't concentrate on listening to the head of the design team because my mind was held hostage by her. For the past month, I'd staked out her apartment, job, and places she liked to hang out. Doing a background check and finding out her last relationship was three years ago worked in my favor. Even if she was with him now, it would not last once I made my intentions known. People could call me a stalker for watching her and wanting to know everything about her. My goal was to know what made her tick, how she thought, what motivated her. Everything that was Emersyn Randolph had every piece of my mind occupied, from her short thick frame, curvy hips, and full lips, up to her round, shapely brown eyes. Her small button nose, even her delicate ears with the three rings on each side that showed her personality. Her smooth, chestnut brown skin intrigued me the most and I wanted the taste of her in my mouth. At my height of five-eleven to her five-five, I could picture lifting her and eating her pussy until she passed out.

"Boss, what do you think?" Sonda, the lead designer of our apps, interrupted my thoughts.

Running a hand down my face, I exhaled a breath, thoughts of how Emersyn tasted still lingering.

I threw my hand up. "Fine, test it out."

All eyes went around the room in shock. I normally was a hard ass on everyone, but today Emersyn somehow made me calm from the small interaction we'd had, and I wanted to be in her presence again. I knew her friends and where they hung out because her friends hung out with my associates, even though we've never been in the same place together. I knew of her, and she'd never met me before nor had the other girls.

"All right, you heard the man. Let's test it out." Sonda's clapping brought me back to the meeting.

I needed to stay focused. Getting my next venture up and making money was my only goal. "How is the work coming for *Passions*? Are we on track for the grand opening?"

"Yes, sir. I spoke with the accountant and the numbers are looking good," my assistant, Benita, relayed. She crossed her legs and leaned forward, showing off her cleavage. I could admit many times I wanted to take her up on her offer of sleeping together, but my father taught me the biggest mistake a man can make was mixing business with pleasure.

"Good. Send over the updates, and Benita? Make sure you pick up a better wardrobe that covers up your skin. I wouldn't want you giving off the wrong impression."

Poking her lip out, she waited as the last person walked out of the conference room and glared at me. "Why do you continue to dismiss me, Esteban?" she demanded, stomping her feet.

I stuffed my hands in my pants pockets. "You were hired to do a job, nothing more."

"You've slept with other employees here."

"Who?"

Her mouth opened and closed. "Well, the girls have talked."

I gestured around the room. "Have I said who I've slept with at my company?"

She lowered her eyes, still pouting. "No," she mumbled under her breath.

"Then it shouldn't matter what some gossiping group has told you. Besides, I would never sleep with you."

Air eked from her throat, as shock swept across her face. "Why not?"

"Because you can't keep your mouth closed long enough to even suck my dick." I marched out, headed back to my office, and was pissed I had to deal with another one of her tantrums. The only woman who could get my attention and have me apologizing was Emersyn Randolph, with the chestnut brown skin, long wavy curls, and full lips. Slamming the door behind me, I slouched down into the seat. I logged into my camera app and focused on Emersyn at work. The smile on her face gave me pause as she laughed at something the guy in front of her said. Biting my lip, I had to control my temper and not go find him and kick his ass like the last guy she went on a date with. Some idiot she had dinner with two months ago who expected to get sex. After she broke up with him, I followed him home and gave him a little message about staying away from what belonged to me. Emersyn didn't know it yet, but she was my future wife and I planned on making sure her every want and need was fulfilled when she became Mrs. Munoz. Wrapping up the details of the *Passions* club opening, I replied to some emails and read over a possible business idea when the door opened. Benita stood in the doorway holding a tight smile.

"Esteban, I have your next meeting here." She stepped to the side, and Remington Falls stepped forward, stretching a hand toward me. We had become friends after I donated to his campaign. I liked what I had learned about his policies and how he wanted to clean up the city. We'd had a love for cigars, and he introduced me to the billionaire boys' club that his friend, Gerald, owned. After going through extensive background checks and becoming an official member, we often ran in the same circles in business and politics.

"Take a seat," I offered, sliding close to my desk.

"Do you need anything to drink, Mr. Senator?" Benita checked, standing too close to Remington. Normally I would fire someone for their constant flirting. Unfortunately, Benita was good at her job and kept things running when I wasn't around.

"Actually, yes, thank you," Remington responded, ignoring her flirtation.

"That will be all, Benita."

Benita swished out of my office. I sat back in my chair and sighed. I needed to decide if she was worth having around for much longer.

"Your assistant is barking up the wrong tree," Remington chuckled, unbuttoning his suit jacket.

"I know."

"She's like that with you?" His brows knitted together, and he frowned at her aggressiveness.

Groaning, I rubbed a hand down my face. "What brings you by?" I wanted to get back to checking on Emersyn and everyone and their mom was in my way.

"I got your invitation from the night club, and I wanted to check on you and see how business was going."

Remington as a senator meant technically we were on opposite sides of things. As a business owner I felt like some of the things politicians did were the same as corrupt businessmen, but he tried to make it all about helping the public.

"Business is business. How are things with you and your wife?"

"Good. I wanted to catch up with you about the news segment about the club and some of the worries that the counsel is having."

Grunting, I knew there was a reason for him to check up on me. "It's not a sex club."

"Esteban, I'm not stupid. As your friend and as a senator, I need to know it's legit."

I scratched my chin. "A small section I do plan on building in a year or two will be set up for adult only themes. For now, it's a regular night club. Part of the opening night profits will be donated to charity."

"That's all it is?"

Leaning forward, I locked my hands together. "What did you think I was going to do?"

His amusement filled eyes dared me to question him. "Honestly, I thought your ass was running an undercover sex ring."

The both of us burst into laughter at his suggestion. "Brother, I do a lot of business, but not that type."

"How will you navigate that with your family's name?"

I shrugged. Originally, I wanted to have a night club as the stomping ground for my business. With all the news stories and social media commentary, people knew me as a single billionaire playboy, and I loved being in control. Having a place built for people to enjoy that lifestyle was a money maker. *Passions* would be a prime location.

"You should have it connected to the cigar bar," Remington said.

"Gerald knows about your suggestion?"

He waved me off. "He would be the perfect person to partner with. The amount of traffic that comes into the bar will benefit you both."

I ran an impatient hand through my hair. "Maybe," I mumbled.

"Are you planning on bringing someone to the opening?"

"I have my pick already," I said with a wide grin on my face.

"Who?" Remington asked, his brow crinkled in confusion.

"Emersyn."

Remington choked on his glass of water. "Emersyn, as in Sanya's friend?"

I laughed and rose to grab the box of tissues from the couch and cleaned up the spill on my desk. "I talked to her in person."

"Emersyn's a sweet girl. Try not to fuck it up. Sanya will drag all of us into your fight."

Remington knew I never put my personal business out for everyone to comment on, so if anything changed with Emersyn and me, they'd be the last to know. My dating reputation wasn't the best. I usually only called women up for specific events to have on my arm. Later I'd treat them to a night with me and send them away until the next time.

"Only fight I plan on having is where Emersyn is going to be sleeping at night."

Remington got up from the chair. "All right, Mr. Suave, are you coming to the bar?" He lifted his cell phone to check the time.

Closing down my computer, I finished cleaning up the mess on my desk. "No votes you need to look at?"

"I have the rest of the afternoon free. My baby is making dinner for us tonight."

Chuckling that the single life no longer concerned him, I was partially proud of him. On the other hand, I wondered how his career would be if he was still single in politics.

Throwing my keys in my pocket, I picked up my phone and walked out behind him, laughing at one of his jokes.

* * *

Stirring my glass of stiff Scotch, I threw my head back in laughter as Gerald and Remington went back and forth about their women. Sanya came out of the back with a few employees, talking and motioning around the room.

Gerald sat up and sipped his glass of rum and coke. "You need a place to get customers for the sex club?"

"Remington offered up your place."

"The club can be reserved for the interview process if you need a place less crowded," Gerald responded.

"Thanks."

"So, what woman has your mind preoccupied?" Gerald gestured to get a refill. One of the bottle girls stepped over and poured another drink for all of us.

Lighting my cigar, I pushed out the smoke. The tension in my body eased and I replayed my meeting with Emersyn. I took out my phone and sent a text to my team to get her number, even though she refused I had ways of making things happen. I planned on spending my life with Emersyn.

Me: I need the number asap Emersyn Randolph.

Eric: Yes Mr. Munoz.

Eric worked for me on private matters outside of my company for the past few years. He was trustworthy, and I got her number just ten minutes later. My smile spreads across my face as I send my text message.

Me: *How is your day?*

Future girl: *Who is this?*

I grimaced at her response.

Me: *Your future. It's Esteban.*

Future girl: I highly doubt you can tell the future.

Me: *Are you free for dinner?*

Future girl: *No.*

Ignoring her response, I put the cigar out in the ashtray and took another sip of Scotch. "Where has your mind gone?" Gerald questioned.

"Emersyn." I sent another text, and I told her I would pick her up for dinner tonight after I left here.

Closing out of the text thread, I heard a familiar voice.

Emersyn.

She looked beautiful standing with Sanya and the bartender near the employee door.

"What am I supposed to say?" Emersyn asked.

I stood up, ignoring Gerald and Remington calling my name. I marched over to Sanya, with Emersyn's back to me.

"Can I help you?" Sanya wondered.

I tapped Emersyn on the shoulder. She turned and gasped in surprise. "Say yes."

Emersyn glanced around the bar. "Esteban, what are you doing here?"

"You know him?" Sanya inquired.

Emersyn blew a heavy sigh. "This is Esteban, the guy I told you about from the other night."

Shyness appeared on her face again, and I was ready to put her concerns to rest.

"How did you get my number?" She asked.

"I have my ways."

Chapter 3

Emersyn

When Sanya told me we had to come to the cigar bar before we headed to lunch, I said fine. Since Louise gave me the rest of today off, I had planned on doing a few video blogs of my book picks for the week. The second my phone chimed with a text, I thought it was joke at first. But when I realized it was Esteban, I felt completely nervous all over again. His offer of dinner surprised me since he was a big-time businessman who could have any woman of his dreams.

"Aren't you friends with Gerald?" Sanya quizzed him.

Esteban focused on me while I looked everywhere except at him. Sucking in a tight breath, my stomach knotted, and I felt lightheaded.

"We are. He talks about you all the time," Esteban responded.

"Nice to meet you. Emersyn, I need to sign off on some papers. We can leave in a few minutes."

"Wait, Sanya!" I snatched her arm to stop her from leaving me alone with him.

Sanya giggled at my distress, patted my hand, and walked toward the back. "Are you nervous, beautiful?" Esteban took a step forward, crowding my space.

I exhaled a long breath. "No."

"Good. I expected to see you at dinner, but I'm happy to see you here."

Being near him gave me a reprieve, but at the same time I grew hot and nervous. "Are you a member?"

"I am."

"Oh."

He pushed his hands into the pockets of his slacks. "Is that a problem?"

"Men like you, I expect you to be here." I pitched my shoulders up as I answered.

He held a hand to his chest in offense. "Men like me?"

"Rich, handsome, egotistical men wanting the girl that frolics behind his every word."

He smiled at my statement. "Only person I plan on frolicking behind is you." He pulled on my braids and licked his lips.

A quiver trickled up my back. "Esteban."

"We have plans for dinner. I want you to dress up."

"I can't."

"Why not?"

"I have a boyfriend," I blurted out. What was I saying? I couldn't believe myself.

He hunched his shoulders. "He's not included in the date."

"Esteban, you and I have nothing in common."

"There will be something in common for us."

"Like what?"

He lifted my chin. "Dinner tonight."

"I can't. I have work."

Grumbling and taking a step back, he relented. "I will give you tonight, but I'm coming for you, Emersyn, and when you're mine all of this running is over." Dipping down low, he kissed me on the cheek. I closed my eyes and inhaled his cologne. My hands automatically went to his chest before he pulled back.

"Answer your phone when I call."

Esteban stalked away from me. I watched him speak with Gerald and leave a few seconds later. I turned to see Sanya standing with a wide shit eating grin on her face.

"Esteban and Emersyn sitting in the tree," Sanya sang.

"Shut up," I huffed, heading out to our cars to leave for lunch. Starting the car, I turned down the radio and put my phone on silent as I drove with my mind on every-thing that happened the other night and today. Esteban's presence intimidated me for some reason, not that I was insecure or hated myself. I was beautiful, smart, and funny, but he's a large personality, a little dark and sexy, the types I had read about in my romance books.

Turning off the block not even ten minutes later, I parked outside of the corner restaurant not far from the bar. I put my car in park, removed the keys, and picked up my purse. I climbed out and I noticed Sanya at the door talking to the doorman.

"Finally, we can talk about your little boyfriend," Sanya teased, stretching her arm around my neck. We both thanked the doorman and stared at the empty lounge she had picked out.

"Three for lunch, under Sanya," she explained to the hostess who grabbed the menus and showed us to our table.

"Who else is meeting us?" I asked. I placed my purse on the back of my seat and scooted my chair up to the table.

"Raya is on her way." Sanya lifted the menu, and I took the other one from the hostess.

"Your waitress will be right over to you," the hostess conveyed, and we thanked her.

"How is Raya doing?"

Dropping the menu on the table, Sanya grabbed her purse and took out a mirror to look herself over. "Great, in love and happy with Remington."

Before I could reply, our waitress appeared, filled our glasses with water, and pulled out a notepad. "Hi, I know you're waiting on one more person," she said.

"Oh, here she comes right now." Sanya waved over my shoulder, and I turned to look. I smiled, remembering Raya from dinner at Sanya's house.

"Hi, ladies, sorry for being late. My car broke down and Remington fussed about me not using the detail." Raya groaned and scanned the menu as we ordered.

"Remington was at the bar before we came here," Sanya mentioned. Taking a sip of water, I listened to the girls go back and forth about their work schedules.

"Okay, enough about work. Emersyn, tell us about you and Esteban." Sanya smirked while sipping her drink.

I shifted in my seat. "I don't know him."

Sanya and Raya snickered together. "Esteban is cute. Why wouldn't you go out with him?"

"Because I'm busy and he's like some rich guy that can have anyone he wants."

No way would I confess I thought Esteban was extremely handsome and made me nervous just by the look in his eyes. I could just ignore his call and hopefully he would forget about me.

"He's friends with Gerald and Remington, so I think he's a good man," Sanya rambled, moving her empty plate out of the way.

"Have you two figured out what book you are reading next?"

"Trying to change the subject." Sanya winked, and Raya giggled at me rolling my eyes.

My fingers gripped the cold glass of water. I gulped down the last drop and then finished my food. "Nothing about my love life needs to change."

"What love life?" Sanya quizzed.

Glaring at her, I ignored her question. "He did ask me out on a date," I mumbled under my breath.

"A date," Raya teased, rubbing her hands together. Sanya grinned and folded her arms across her chest.

"I did not accept."

The girls shrieked in confusion. "He's single, right?" Sanya pondered, to my annoyance.

"Yes."

"Then what's the problem?"

I shook my head. "Just tired of being disappointed."

"Honey, you have to go through some frogs before you get your prince," Raya reminded me, removing money from her wallet to split the check. All three of us stood and hugged goodbye, going in different directions for the rest of the night.

* * *

Avoiding Esteban for the past week worked out great for a little while. A few times he called me and texted. I basically played it off because of how busy work had been for me. Some people thought working in a bookstore was easy, but it could be time consuming on top of being the best job I have ever had. Saturday finally rolled around, and the girls were meeting me at our favorite coffee shop to talk about plans for our next book club reading. Walking up to the register, my favorite barista, Jonathan, stood at the counter. He picked up the sharpie and cup to write down my drink order. For the past year, if I wasn't with Sanya, the shop had become my second favorite place to hang out. It helped that it was between my place and the bookstore.

"How are you, Emersyn? Long time, no see," Jonathan emphasized, smiling at me.

"Hi, Johnathan. I know! I'm so sorry, but today I'm finally able to run errands and hang out with the girls."

Jonathan slid the cup over to the bar. "You know we missed you around here."

I reached into my purse to grab my wallet, but I tensed when a hand wrapped around my wrist. "On me. Let me get a large black coffee, one sugar."

Esteban reached around my waist with his chest to my back and dropped a twenty-dollar bill on the counter. Jonathan glanced between me and Esteban. I hesitated before turning toward Esteban with a hard glare.

"I can pay for my own drink."

"Why? When I'm around, you pay for nothing."

Planting my hands on my hips, I scoffed at his cocky demeanor. "You are not my boyfriend."

His top lip curved, and he smirked as he bit down on his bottom lip and stared at me.

"Uh, Emersyn, do you know this guy?" Jonathan called out.

A flash of a frown on his face disappeared after a second, and I wondered why Esteban would be mad at Jonathan.

"She's of no concern to you." Esteban cupped my elbow and pulled me over to the side.

I snatched away from him. "What are you doing?"

"Taking care of my girl."

Chuckling at his comment, I turned to ignore his presence and picked up my iced latte from the counter and looked around for a table.

"What are you doing?"

"Since you never answered my calls, I thought we could have the date here," Esteban insisted.

Poking out my lip, I rolled my eyes, sat back, and opened my Kobo reader. "My friends are coming, so you should leave before they get here." I searched the store in anticipation for Sanya to get here.

"They're not coming."

"What?"

"Sanya and Raya aren't coming."

I nibbled on my top lip. "How do you know?"

"I talked to them about our date."

I blew out a breath. "Esteban, we are not dating, boyfriend and girlfriend, or any type of relationship," I told him as I lifted my drink to take a sip.

"One date and I will leave you alone."

"Fine," I acquiesced. My mouth pressed into a thin line.

Standing up, he stretched his hand out to me. "Right now."

I choked on my drink. "Right now?" No way. Was he serious?

"But I'm not dressed for a date! I planned on running some errands and hanging with my friends."

"You look fine to me."

I looked down at my blue jeans, crop top, and sandals. My hair was an uncontrolled mess in a silky wrap.

"Emersyn, anything you wear only enhances your beauty."

He held the door open, and we stepped out of the coffee shop. I was astonished to see a stretch limo waiting. "Please tell me that's not your ride."

"Emersyn, I will never apologize for my wealth."

I couldn't help but roll my eyes. "I didn't ask you to."

"Then let's go." He waited for me to climb in, then he followed, sitting close to me. I picked up my ringing phone to see Sanya's incoming call.

"Yes, Sanya," I dragged out, hearing her laugh hysterically.

"Sorry, babe. He called Gerald to get my number," Sanya said.

"I hate you."

"No, you love me. Enjoy yourself and give him a chance."

Out the corner of my eye, I could see Esteban watching me on the phone.

I sighed heavily. I took in what she said. There was no way Esteban was going to just go away. So, this once, I would stop fighting his attempts to see me. Besides, it wouldn't go anywhere after this one date.

"Call me later, Sanya."

"Bye, babe, and remember to let him spoil you." Giggling, she hung up, and I started to put the phone away when Esteban took it out of my hands.

"Hey!"

He wiggled his finger in my face. "I get you all to myself."

"Says who?"

"No distractions, Emersyn. Relax and let me get to know you." Esteban's driver stopped in front of a gallery.

"What are we doing here?"

"We're going to check out some pieces I need for my house, and I know you love art."

"Who told you I loved art?"

He stepped out of the car. He smirked and offered me his hand. "Come on, we have the place for the next hour."

I pointed at the hours on the door. "It's closed."

"Yep, I know the owner and he let me have the place for our date."

Esteban held the door to the gallery open and I stepped in, glancing around at the African art pieces on the wall. The textures mesmerized me, the layers of each story gave me peace, and I wanted to know more of what the artist was thinking.

"These are beautiful," I whispered as I glanced at the descriptions on the wall for each piece.

"To me art is like a great book. Each one tells a story either to escape or to reminisce," he revealed before grasping my hand and moving me along to the next area. For over an hour we talked about how he met Roman, the owner of the gallery, years ago because of their families doing business together.

"Thank you for bringing me here," I told him.

Esteban locked up the building before we headed to the car and jumped into the back. We settled into our seats, and he interlocked our hands.

"That's the first part of our date." Smirking, he lifted our hands and gently placed a kiss on the back of mine.

Chapter 4

Esteban

Taking Emersyn on a date had been the plan from the moment we met, but I knew getting her to agree would be hard based on our first meeting. Sanya and Gerald helped me to understand Emersyn's personality. I learned from her best friend that she never cared for the big flashy money that most guys would throw her way. My goal was to show her I wanted to get to know the real her and she would give me a chance that I knew we both needed. No man would come along after me, and I for damn sure had no plans of leaving her alone. She was mine. Taking her to the park for a meal would be spontaneous and out of the norm. Flicking the lights on surrounding the gazebo in the park, I pulled the chair back for her to take a seat.

I knew she secretly loved my attention and admired my efforts. "How were you able to get the park to allow us here?"

"I have my secrets." The sun going down gave us the perfect setting.

"Esteban, you've outdone yourself."

"Emersyn, when I said I wanted you, I meant it." I opened the bottle of wine to pour into her glass, then mine.

Her face flushed with embarrassment. "I feel under-dressed."

"You look beautiful to me."

"Tell me, Esteban, why me?"

"Why not you? I'm obsessed with you, Emersyn. Your smile, your laugh, your thoughtfulness."

Shyness crept into her face at my compliments. "Thank you."

"I come from a very well-known family. As I stated before, my wealth is something I will never apologize for, but you will always know where I stand."

"Tell me about your upbringing."

"I was a normal kid, growing up with expectations to run the family business. I'm an only child."

"I'm the only child in my family too. That's why Sanya and I are close."

Their friendship meant a lot to her, and I see that because of the protectiveness they have with each other.

"She promised to kick my ass if I hurt you," I told her, recalling my conversation with Sanya. She snickered.

"Sanya's like a big sister to me."

At some point Emersyn would meet my parents and become my wife. I would go along with dating, but she would never need another man.

"Are you sure you want to pursue me? I mean, I don't look like the women you normally date."

I knew I was being talked about in the society papers and social media had tried to create the narrative of me as a playboy womanizer. "Stay off the gossip blogs, Emersyn. No one knows what I like."

She cut into her food, and as she lifted the fork to her mouth, a little bit of the cream from the sauce dropped to her cheek. I swiped the remaining sauce with my finger, sticking it in my mouth.

"Sweet."

"Esteban," she moaned.

"I'm not playing with you, Emersyn. I want you." Dropping my napkin on the table, I covered her hand with mine.

"We can try. I haven't dated in a few months."

"I want more than a few months."

"You are not the slow type of guy with dating I see." Amusement etched her face.

"Slow in certain places and at certain times, like when I take your sweet lips into my mouth, or when I'm sucking on your pearl." I slowly teased my fingers across her wrist.

"Esteban." She sheepishly looked around the quiet park that was normally filled with crowds of people, as if she expected someone could hear my dirty desires. Darkness had started to fall, and I wanted to continue our conversation, but I didn't want to push her too much.

I could see my words were making her come undone. I watched her crossing and uncrossing her legs, rubbing the back of her neck, avoiding eye contact. "Do you want me, Emersyn?"

"Yes."

"Do you want me to fuck you, Emersyn?"

She purred softly and gulped her wine. "Yes, Esteban."

"Take your finger and play with your pussy."

Whispering, she checked her surroundings. "I can't," she whimpered and then checked again to see who might have been around to hear me and my demands.

I removed the glass from in front of her. She sat up in the chair, squirming under my watchful eyes. "Yes, you can and yes, you will."

"We're in public."

"How wet are you, Emersyn?"

She flushed at my words, but Emersyn still obeyed me and slowly pushed her finger in her pants, closed her eyes, and moaned.

My wandering eyes were laser focused on her. "Let me taste you, baby."

Her smile became warm and dreamy. "Oh, god..."

"He's not here right now. Only me and you."

"I want you, too, Esteban."

"Then come home with me now and understand it's non-negotiable."

"What does that mean?"

"It means I want to consume you, please you. Make you mine," I growled, sinking my hands onto her hips. I peppered kisses down her neck and squeezed her ass.

"Take me home."

* * *

Swiveling her eyes to mine as we approached my bedroom door, Emersyn took in the black and crimson sheets, the tasteful artwork on the walls and my large king size bed and mirror above the ceiling.

"You have a beautiful home." Emersyn walked toward the edge of the bed, but she stopped and turned to me with lust filled eyes.

I slid off my jacket and unbuttoned my shirt. I kept my eyes on her and watched her gaze as she roamed from my face to the tent in my pants.

"I can give you a better tour tomorrow."

Her cheeks blushed and she looked down, then kicked off her shoes. "What makes you think I will be here that long?" Stepping closer to me, she cupped the back of my neck.

I ran a hand under her chin and sighed heavily. "Are you planning on leaving after I give you the best orgasms of your life?"

She licked her plump lips. "No. But I wonder... how long will it take before you move on?"

"Never."

"Never?"

"I could never move on from you, sweetheart. Lie down on the bed, baby. Slowly."

Keeping eye contact with me, Emersyn stuck her hands inside her jogging pants, moving them down her curvy hips and thick thighs. Lifting her top off, I stopped her from undoing her bra.

"Let me do the honor."

I eased my arms around her back and kissed a trail down her neck and shoulders. I felt a chill when her hand grazed against my dick.

I strode forward, planting both hands on her hips. "Keep teasing me and see what happens."

"Please fuck me, Esteban."

Capturing her swollen breasts in my hands, I watched her response flit across her face. I stared at her as I played with my favorite new toys. Spreading her legs wide, I lowered my head and glided her panties down her legs then pushed my nose to her center and smelled.

"Perfection."

She tried to please herself, and I smacked her hand away with a harsh glare.

"That's my job now."

"Nothing like the books. My book bae would have fucked her by now," she grumbled with a frown, and I chuckled.

"Don't compare me to your little book boyfriends."

I teased her breasts, my lips hovering over her mouth before we made eye contact. "Fuck me, Esteban."

"Yes, ma'am."

Gazing down at her luscious lower lips, the silky soft skin shivered under my touch. This wasn't how I expected our date to end up, but she more than wanted to be here with me. The first time I saw her had me mesmerized. To be in her presence no matter what was the only goal. Once I left, she blocked me on the phone that very day. Getting her to understand I wasn't some playboy that only wanted sex became my mission. I loved our talks, seeing her at work and finding out I could be myself without all of the headaches that come with my last name. I heard her moans and purrs of pleasure as I dove my tongue into her warmth. Emersyn arched her back off the bed. I tried to keep her from moving too much, but seeing her reckless with her movements showed I was giving her the best oral pleasure of her life.

"Esteban!" Emersyn screamed. Hearing my name from her lips, I sped up my movements, drowning in her juices. She flooded my sheets with her essence, and I came up for air. I kissed her, sticking my tongue in her mouth, letting her grip both sides of my face.

"Taste yourself, baby. You ready for more?"

Flicking her nipples, she nodded. I loved it when she talked about the things that excited her, from the mundane to her favorite books. My senses were spun by the scent of her arousal, and I eased my hands down to cup her pussy. Lowering my head to kiss each nipple, she was fully aware of the hardness sitting between her legs.

"Stop playing with me," she grumbled. I liked when her feistiness came out. I pinched her nipples and slid my dick into her entrance and thrust forward.

"Hmmmm...." she cooed, her voice trembling low.

My mind flashed to us in twenty years, married with kids going off to college and having the house to ourselves. Wanting a marriage and family had never been a part of my future plans, but Emersyn had changed everything I set for myself.

I gripped both of her luscious breasts and pulled her close to me, as I eased in and out of her body. Her cries filled the room. I slapped her thigh gently. Seeing the little jiggle confirmed her full curves kept me on edge. I pumped faster to keep her on a high and wanting more, but then slowed back down as she tried to tug me closer to feel her heart beating faster.

"Esteban, right there. Yesss!"

Desperate to keep her underneath me for a while longer, I closed my eyes, picturing her carrying my first born son and breastfeeding him.

"Fuck! Eme...baby, you feel so good."

I nuzzled my nose into her neck, smelling her vanilla scent, and lightly bit her on the neck, licking the sting away.

I slammed into her, but pulled back out, not ready to come. Her eyes snapped in my direction as I moved closer to the edge of the bed.

"What are you doing?"

"Not ready for you to come, baby."

She lifted onto her elbows. "Why are you playing?" she whined. I grasped her by her ankles until she sat up straight with her feet flat on the floor, her legs spread wide. I spit on her pussy and pushed my tongue back inside.

"Ughhh...Shit, go deeper."

"Good girl, stay still."

Riding my face, Emersyn got a good rhythm going. I made her not only my main course, but dessert and late night snack, sucking the last drop from her sweet nectar.

Easing my leg on the side of her, I bent my leg a little. I pressed all the way back so deeply, it felt as if our bodies were locked as one.

"Fuck! You're drowning the bed, baby."

She turned to face me. "Make me come, Esteban," she cooed, arching her ass up a little, making me sink even further.

Against all logic, I felt a need to claim her body after claiming her mind. I closed my eyes, hearing her screams, our skin slapping together, and feeling the tingling at the base of my dick. I was ready to fill her with my kids. I didn't care about not having a real commitment. I knew she would have my last name one day.

"Arghhhhh! Emersyn. Fuck, come for me."

Her head fell back, eyes tight as we both came at the same time. We were both out of breath and sweaty, and I was ready to go for another round. But we needed to refuel our bodies. I pulled her back to my chest, not wanting our bodies to be separated even by the slightest inch. I kissed the side of her neck and grabbed a fistful of her hair. The instant she covered my hand on top of her pussy, my dick hardened again.

"Let's eat something before I take you again."

Her hazy eyes gazed up at me. "What about the tour?"

"Tomorrow. First, I want to tour more of your body."

She cackled and I grasped her hand, walking out of my bedroom down the hall to the kitchen. For the next hour we ate some of the leftovers from dinner, showered, and fucked again before falling asleep.

Chapter 5

Emersyn

month later.

Yawning, I could barely keep my eyes open from another night at Esteban's, where he gave me another tour of his bedroom and eventually we headed to his club and hung out. He had to sign a few papers and I stayed in the back watching from the cameras. At one point the girls came and we drank and danced a little while the men hung together. When he told me we were official, I wanted to tell him to slow down, but being on a specific timeline never mattered to him and I liked feeling the freedom of just going with the flow.

"Emersyn, did you hear me?" Louise asked.

It was a brisk sunny day, so I had decided to walk to work. "Sorry, I'm tired. What did you say?"

Louise drew nearer, grabbing her drink. "Are you alright?"

"Exhausted, long night," I said with a heavy sigh. I cracked my neck.

"Would it have anything to do with a Mr. Esteban?"

I loaded more change in the cash register. "Maybe." I rang up a few pre-orders and packed them.

"I like him for you."

I bagged up a few more books. "He's okay."

"Okay? Girl, that man has you wide open."

Laughing, I waved her off. "Louise, nobody has me open."

"Please. I know a girl in love."

"He's alright." I extended my hand to take a few books out of her hand.

"Sure, Jane," Louise jokes.

The front door dinged, alerting someone was coming in. I moved my coffee to the back counter and smiled at the flower arrangement.

"Well, I know I haven't done anything to receive flowers," Louise said with a loud laugh.

"Looking for Emersyn Randolph," the delivery driver requested as he put the flowers on the counter.

"That's me." I picked up the card to read. *Be ready at eight, baby. Esteban.* Giving the driver a tip, I took in the red and yellow roses.

Louise stickered a stack of books. "Like I told you, wide open."

"Is it weird to have these intense feelings with him so fast?"

"Only if he's giving you red flags. But from what you've said, everything is flowing well."

"They are, and my last relationship was nothing like me and Esteban."

She winked her left eye at me with a grin. "A relationship. He makes it easy to just be you."

"Yes, sweet hangover."

"So happy for you, Emersyn. Love looks good on you."

"Thanks, Louise."

She taps her hands on the counter. "Since he wants you ready by eight, you can leave early today and I can lock up."

I clasped my hands together and leaned forward. "I can't do that."

"Yes, you can."

"Are you sure?"

Louise strolled to the back. "Yep, enjoy that man."

"Thanks. I got the next customer."

Ringing up two more customers, I filled my time doing inventory for the next few hours and listening to Sanya complain on the phone about Gerald and the cigar bar. Finally six pm came around and Louise nearly pushed me out of the shop to get home and get ready for my date with my man. Tonight I had no real idea of where we would go so I decided to put on a simple jumpsuit and heels with a little neckline showing off my cleavage, a little foundation, and lipstick.

He arrived at my place promptly at eight. Shutting the door behind me, Esteban took my hand and led me to the car.

"Where's the limo?"

"Tonight I wanted to drive you myself."

"Really, just the two of us?"

He unlocked the door of his Bentley. "You and me alone."

Stepping forward, I placed my hand on his chest. "Thank you."

He locked his arm around my waist, then smacked my

ass gently. "Thank me when I have you bent over the dinner table eating your pussy."

"Terrible, Mr. Esteban."

He laughed loudly. I watched him walk around to get in on the driver's side, put my seatbelt on, and clasped my hands together.

"Where are we going exactly?"

"I thought I could treat you to a little trip."

Relaxing in the warm seats, I asked, "Trip?" Staring at his side profile, it gave off an aura to let him take me here and now.

"Yeah, have you been to a cabin?"

Living in New York, I mostly stayed in and around the city, Times Square, Brooklyn, and the Bronx. Going out to the woods never really popped into my mind. "No, but isn't it a little cold around this time to be up in the woods?"

He put the key in the ignition and started the engine. "My property won't be cold," he assured me as he got on the road.

"What about work?"

He patted his phone. "I can work from anywhere."

"How long will we be gone?" I asked. We moved through the streets, listening to cars, people yelling and cursing each other out leaving my place.

"Just a day or two."

"But I have no clothes with me."

"I can get you whatever you need." I stared at him as he stopped at the light, pulled out his cell, and sent a message.

Making a last minute trip kind of pissed me off, especially not knowing what I had planned for work or if I needed to be in the city. "What about my job?"

"Louise knows you will be gone for the weekend."

I leaned against the window. "You thought of every-thing. What if I said no?"

Wrapping a hand around my neck, he kissed me while ignoring the honking of the cars behind us. "You wouldn't pass up me fucking you all night long."

"True." I giggled, laying a hand on his thigh.

Hours later we arrived at the sanctuary that he used to get away from the city for peace and alone time with his family. I marveled at the exquisite three story mansion, not a small cabin like I had thought. The place sat on acres of land filled with beautiful trees and a lake in the back, along with ducks and a boat. After escorting me through the kitchen, we moved toward the fridge that was filled with food. A bar sat in the corner. A large fireplace and more artwork surrounded the place.

"You have a beautiful place here." I sipped on a glass of wine as I stood in front of the fireplace.

"Come have a seat next to me."

"What about dinner?"

"It's almost ready."

Another thing that surprised me—Esteban could cook. Watching him in his apron stirring a sweet sauce for the pasta with his sleeves rolled up turned me on more than him being shirtless. A man who could cook and fuck was a perfect combination.

Plopping down on the couch, I laid my head on his shoulder while he ran a hand up and down my thigh. "How are you feeling?"

"Good."

"I know we went fast, but I know when I want something I go full speed ahead."

"No...really... I never noticed," I joked.

He tapped me on the nose. "Next thing is meeting your parents and mine."

"How are you so sure?"

"Because I know you want me and see your future with me, Emersyn. Time has no place in our dynamic."

"Sounds like a man that knows what he wants."

"Definitely know I want you."

"Glad to hear you want me, so let's eat and then we can have dessert."

Groaning, he stood and fixed himself then took me by the hand to the dining room to take a seat. A few moments later, plates of food came out, and we were ready to dive into his favorite dishes.

"After dinner we can watch a movie, and tomorrow we're going out on my boat."

"So, we're on a little mini vacation/date?"

"Is that a problem? Me spoiling you?"

"At first, I had some doubts if you would use your money to get me to fall for you, but you've shown me a side of yourself that really wants to get to know me as a person and not flaunt money at me."

"We have plenty of time to spoil you, but for now, I like our talks and you showing me the other side of Emersyn."

"What side is that?"

"The side of you taking my dick in your mouth, and my cum dripping out of your pussy."

"Esteban." Those words always kept me blushing.

We finished dinner and moved to the theater. He turned on the movie, while I kicked off my heels. I sat close to him under the covers, and we watched *Pretty Woman*. A few hours later I felt around my body. I was completely nude, and I gasped at the feel of his lips on my pussy. Sometime in the middle of the evening, I probably fell asleep in his arms, and he carried me to bed. The smell of his sweet musky cologne drifted through the air around us. My stomach dropped as I sucked in a breath, and his hands slid up to cup my breasts.

"Tell me what you want me to do, Emersyn."

"I want you to fuck me."

Esteban leaned up, peppering kisses along my thighs. With a smirk on his face, he nibbled on my mound, hovered over my body, and crushed his mouth to mine.

I trembled under his steady gaze. I closed my eyes tight. I would never get over how big he was when he's on top.

"Mmmmhhh...We have plans tomorrow, so I think you should get some rest." Esteban cupped my chin, pecked my lips, and moved to the other side of the bed. Then he wrapped me in his arms.

"Are you serious?"

Closing his eyes, he nodded. "I just wanted a taste," he said with a satisfied smirk.

I tried to move out of his grip, but he snatched me closer and smacked me on the ass. "Stop."

"Stop teasing me, please..." I hated to whine, but the liquid seeping down my legs would only get worse if I couldn't release. Esteban roamed a hand up and down my back and pressed a kiss to my forehead.

"If you go to sleep now, I promise to give you more orgasms tomorrow after the boat ride."

"What if I want to skip the boat ride?"

Turning over to spoon me from behind, he ran a hand up and down my arm and leg.

"Tomorrow, you can ride me all night long baby. Get some sleep."

* * *

The early morning sunlight beamed brightly into the bedroom. I pushed the covers over my head, not wanting to get up. For the first time in a long while I slept like a baby snuggled in Esteban's arms, listening to his soft snores.

Smack!

Jumping up in annoyance, I rubbed my ass. "Esteban!" I chided. I shoved the covers back and pushed my feet into the house shoes he had purchased for me. I angrily grabbed the robe on the back of the door.

"Time for you to get up."

"It's not even seven thirty yet!"

"Whenever I come out here, I like to get up early."

"Why?" Instead of waiting for the answer, I walked into the bathroom, taking the fresh toothbrush and paste so I could get my day started.

"My sanctuary." He came up behind me to nuzzle his head in between my shoulders. Esteban went to turn on the shower. I glanced at him through the mirror, watching his muscles flex, and his rod stick up through his boxers.

Spitting out the toothpaste, I rinsed my mouth. I sauntered over and stood on tiptoes in front of him. I wound my arms around his neck and sucked on his bottom lip.

"Hop in the shower with me."

"As much as I want to do that, I have breakfast cooking. Get dressed and meet me downstairs."

"You're no fun."

Chuckling, Esteban stretched a hand around my throat. "Fun will come later when you're sitting on my face again."

There was weakness in my legs at his words, making it hard to stand.

"Shower, breakfast, and then boat ride."

"Okay," I responded, in a trance.

Thirty minutes passed by and I loved that he had all my hair products and body washes I'd need to get through the mini vacation. Once dressed in a short set, I went downstairs to sit at the table and watch him clean up the kitchen before joining me to eat.

"You cooked all this food by yourself?"

"Did you think I grew up with maids and butlers?"

I poured syrup on my pancakes. "Yes," I answered.

"You are right! Also, they taught me a few things and my mother made sure I knew how to take care of myself."

"Mmmmm..." I moaned at the sweet taste of chocolate pancakes and sausages.

"Get up. I have the boat fueled up and lunch planned."

Nodding, I got up with him. I was happy to be here and see him out of his normal business suit and tie, more laid back in shorts and a regular shirt like a normal guy.

Chapter 6

Esteban

Spending time alone with Emersyn without any worries, I found myself falling even more deeply in love with her. The time I had planned for us was to be only focused on us and keeping the outside world locked away. She'd been able to see a side of me I hadn't let anyone know about. Hearing her stories of her life with her parents, friends, and school up to now and what she had envisioned for herself made me want to spoil her even more. My money was a sore spot for the most part, but she'd accepted that it didn't run my life, and I'd never use it to buy her love. After packing a lunch and heading out, I grinned when we came to the dock on the lake. Seeing Emersyn's mouth drop open in shock at the boat I had was worth the trip here.

"I thought it was a small little boat. This is like a luxury liner!"

I pulled her hand up to my lips. "I want you to enjoy yourself and lay out on the deck."

"I feel underdressed in my shorts."

"I have your bikini or we can go full nude."

Snickering, Emersyn shook her head. "I knew you were up to something."

"When it pertains to you, always, baby."

I guided her to step onto the boat with my team holding out glasses of champagne. Normally a meal was prepared by a chef, but I cooked a meal for us to enjoy while we sat near the deck. I put the basket down and helped Emersyn to a seat. She settled in with her feet under her legs, drinking the champagne.

"Wow! This place is gorgeous." Emersyn took in the large empty lake, with the birds chirping and trees on the side.

"Do you own all of the property?"

"I do. Is that a problem for you?"

She pushed her braids into a tight bun on top of her head. "Nope, the privacy is good."

"Glad you agree." I pulled her back into my chest. She turned to straddle my lap and kissed me. "What's that for?"

"That is for thinking of me and bringing me here," she answered as she waved her hand around.

Our captain took us out to the middle of the lake. I saw the bright sunshine over the land I purchased without my family's name. I had over ten acres of property and I hoped to gain more land and build another home on the property.

"Tell me your thoughts."

"I'm thinking of you in a wedding dress, your hair exactly like it is now."

Her eyes were wide in her face. "A wedding?"

"Marriage was never in my plan but being with you made me want you forever."

"Forever?" Her lips were only a whisper away from

mine. She lightly caressed my chest, and I moved my hand and gave her ass a light squeeze.

Linking our hands together, I sighed. I felt a calmness having her near me. "What do you want out of life?"

"One day I will have my own business."

"What type of business?"

"A bookstore." She giggled.

"Of course."

"I went to school for physical therapy, got bored, and changed to literature. I tried to do what my parents wanted and decided to change majors."

"Business owner. Huh."

She looped her arm around my neck. "I do want to be married one day and have kids."

I pecked her lips gently, and my dick stirred in my pants, ready for her.

She raised her head. "Do you want a boy or girl?"

"I don't care as long as they're healthy," I responded. "Get up for a minute." I took the glass out of her hand and stood up, grabbing the fishing rod next to us.

"What are you doing with that?"

"Do you know how to fish?"

She crossed her arms. "No."

"I can teach you."

"Wait, a billionaire that likes to go fishing?" She laughed so hard, she had to take a second and then she stood next to me.

"How about we make a bet."

She frowned. "But it's my first time fishing."

"I will teach you and if you win, you get to fall asleep with my mouth on your pussy."

She grazed her hand across my dick. "What if you win?"

"I get to fall asleep with my dick in your ass."

She gasped, looking around to see if anyone heard me. "That would be a first for me."

"I promise to take it easy on you." I smoothly rubbed her ass, and she moaned next to me.

"Fine, but don't cheat."

"Baby, it's my boat."

"So." She pouted and tried to snatch the pole out of my hand.

"Come on, big baby. Get in front of me and hold it with both hands."

"Is that a worm?!" Emersyn shrieked and jumped back, scared.

Holding her in place I helped her cast the line and slowly reel it back in. "Looking good, baby. You're ready to do it alone now."

"You're setting me up," she fussed.

Standing next to her, I picked up my pole and we talked more about what to do when we got back to town and my work schedule with the club opening.

"Baby! I think I got something," Emersyn screeched and lunged forward. I captured her around the waist to help pull the pole back and nothing came up but an empty soda can.

"Nice try. You have twenty more minutes to get something."

Mocking me, she pushed me lightly to the side and tried to take mine from my hand, and I pulled it away as something caught on and I reeled in a catfish.

"Not fair!" Emersyn stomped her feet.

"You lost the bet, but I can compromise."

"How?"

"I let you fall asleep with my face in your pussy, and you with my dick in your mouth."

"How?"

"Time for a sixty-nine, baby."

Chortling, I dropped the catfish in the bin, then walked her to the bathroom to clean up and have lunch before we headed back to the house for a nap and dinner.

* * *

She moaned aloud with erotic pleasure, not disguising her body's reaction. She yielded to her searing need to the buildup of me fucking her sweet pussy. I slurped up all her juices as I flicked my tongue across her slit. Emersyn squeezed her thighs around my head, surrendering completely as her body began to radiate at my seduction. While I consumed her sweet arousal, Emersyn tried to push me away. Her eyes rolled back every so often, so I knew she was ready to explode. I pushed both of her legs back further, dived deeper, and slid the tip of my finger into her other hole. I explored her thighs and moved up to her stomach, pressing kisses, taking small bites. I liked to move between pleasure and pain sometimes. Moving my hands smoothly over her lusty breasts, I encouraged her to spread her legs wider, then held the tip of my cock at her entrance.

She gasped at the thick hardness. "Ohhh," she moaned.

"Tell me, Emersyn. What do you want, baby?"

"I want you," she cried out. "Please." I slowly moved another inch forward. Before I could ask again, she tried to take in more and I pulled out completely.

"What are you doing, little one?"

"Please, Esteban, give it to me," she begged. I ran a thumb across her full lips.

"Open your mouth."

Slowly she stuck her tongue out and I pushed my finger inside. She wrapped her lips around it and stroked the digit like it was my dick.

"Are you hungry for my dick, princess?"

"Yesss!"

Driving my tip back to her entrance, I went in and out at a steady pace as she sucked on my thumb. I felt her get wetter from my dominance and giving her body sensual satisfaction.

"That's right, Emersyn. Take all of me." My woman felt so good I had to grit my teeth. Her cries and tears falling down her cheeks let me know she was ready for more. I pulled out slowly and tapped the head of my dick to her ass. She jumped slightly, and I soothed her with my voice. I extended my hand to the nightstand, grabbing the lube to prep her for entry.

"Shussshhh. Breathe, baby."

"Oh God, Esteban."

I licked the side of her neck and sucked on her puckered nipples. Slowly I pressed against her entrance just a little more. She tensed and I moved back to let her get comfortable with my length.

"Fuck, Emersyn!" Being fully inside of her gave me chills. She probably thought I had control, but she had more control over me than she thought. I wanted this first time having anal play to be special for her and to feel good.

"You, right there."

Slamming back in faster, I was on the brink of giving her all of my cum without a care of her getting pregnant.

Thrashing under my hold, she sank her nails in my back, ready to come as her cries got louder.

"Come for me, Emersyn."

Throwing her head back, her mouth wide open, Emersyn's eyes rolled back as she released all over my dick. I pulled out, feasting on her pussy with my finger slowly thrusting into her ass again.

"Shit." I stroked my dick, releasing my seed all over the bed and her body.

Chapter 7

Emersyn

I poured a glass of wine and sat the tray of food down on the counter. Book club was happening at my place. I promised the girls I wouldn't cancel since all of my time had been spent with Esteban. Even months later we'd been non-stop in each other's space. Somehow, I'd grown attached to hearing from him when he texted me good morning or at night before bed. The man made it his mission to show me I was the one he wanted. Like right now he was in my bedroom showering, getting ready to leave to go hang out with his friends. We spent time at each other's place, and he even told me to leave a few things there. At first, I thought we were moving too fast, but Sanya told me to not question things, just go with the flow. I felt large hands wrap around my waist. I looked down at his long thick fingers. He pecked the back of my neck, then I turned my head and stared up at his smile.

"How was the shower?"

"It would have been better if you joined me."

"If I'd joined you, then I would be late getting ready for the girls to show."

A second later the doorbell rang. He reluctantly released his grip on me. I put the bottle down and walked to the door. I opened to find Sanya and the rest of the book club members had arrived.

"Hey, girl! It smells good here." Sanya passed another bottle of wine to me and took off her coat.

"Thanks. I cooked mashed potatoes, grilled salmon, tomatoes, and vegetables."

"Sounds great. Hey, Esteban." Sanya waved at him.

"He's not staying."

Esteban winked at me and kissed me on the lips. "Have fun, but not too much," he said, smacking me lightly on the butt.

"Call me later," I whispered, watching him leave.

"Alright, he's gone now, so give us the real tea," Raya joked and sat down with a glass of wine in her hand.

I ambled to the table and refilled more cups. "No tea to spill. We're dating."

Sanya picked up a plate and filled it with food. "Seems like you're in love."

"Sanya, we are not you and Gerald."

"He has you all the time. We can barely get you to go out with us."

"Here she goes... Just say you missed me," I jested.

"Looking a little thicker, best friend." Sanya motioned over my body.

"Happy weight."

Sanya cackled, and all I could do was laugh. "Yeah, it's called a good dick."

"Come on. Let's get started on today's book pick."

"I'm so excited to read *Wet Heat* by KeKe Renee," Raya commented.

* * *

Days later I stepped off the elevator at Esteban's office carrying a bag of food. I smiled at the security guards. Esteban had introduced me to some of his staff and invited me to a few work dinners. I wanted to treat him like he'd always treated me from amazing trips to elegant meals, so I decided to surprise him with lunch. I lightly tapped on his door and waited for him to call out so I could enter. His assistant motioned that it was okay. Turning the knob, I smiled at my man sitting behind the desk giving out orders. I placed the bag of food down on the desk, then went back to the door and locked it. Turning back to him, I watched his brow hike up.

"Call me back in an hour."

I removed my trench coat and I was only wearing a short bodycon dress underneath. His eyes turned into slits. "Make that two hours." Esteban hung up the phone, not waiting for an answer.

"Surprise."

He licked his lips and groaned. "You're wearing the shit out of that dress."

I picked up some napkins. "Thank you. Are you hungry?"

"Not for food." He reached to pull me close, and I smacked his hands away.

"Food first."

He cupped my ass again. "I wasn't hungry for food."

"It doesn't matter. You should eat."

"What if I want to eat you?" He pressed his hard length against me.

I snickered at him for misbehaving and moved out of

his grip. I set the food out and took a seat next to him behind the desk.

"How is your day going?"

"Fine."

"Come on, baby. For me, try and care about the food."

Grunting he picked up the plate of Mediterranean food, ate a little, and smiled. "Thank you for coming today."

"You're welcome. Since you surprise me so much, I wanted to do the same for you."

I moved over and sat in his lap. "Tonight I have a little business at the club. You want to join me?"

"I do."

"Sounds like you're stalking me now."

I kissed him on the nose. "Wherever my man goes, I'm there."

"I like the sound of those words."

"That's good to know."

Esteban lifted his fork to feed me. "How was work?"

"I had it off today. Louise said to enjoy my boyfriend."

He quirked his brow. "Boyfriend..."

"Boyfriend until a ring is on my finger."

We laughed and we continued to eat when a knock came at the door. I put away the trash, and he stood, strolled around the desk, and opened the door to let Connor, his Vice President, come inside.

"Lovely Emersyn, so good to see you."

"Hi, Connor." I stuck my hand out, and he picked it up to raise it to his lips. Esteban snatched my hand away, causing us both to laugh.

"He's grumpy today I see." Connor took a seat in front of his desk.

I pointed my finger at him. "Not too much on my man, Connor."

Both chortled and I grinned at seeing his armor come down. "What's up Connor?" Esteban asked.

"Are we still on for the club tonight?" Connor questioned.

"Yeah, and my baby is joining me," Esteban said.

"Are you sure? I know a few clients will be there?" Connor mentioned.

"If it's business, I can go another day."

He yanked me into his lap, and he moved a hand up and down my thigh. "The only thing important is you."

He cupped my chin and we leaned into a kiss. He snaked his tongue into my mouth. I moaned at his smooth touch, and my arousal stirred.

"Guess I should leave you two alone." Connor stood up, walking out of the room as we made out with the door wide open, not caring if anyone saw us.

"Should we finish at home?" I asked.

"Are you wearing panties?" Esteban slipped his hand in between my thighs.

"No."

"Bad girl, Emersyn."

"I like being bad for you."

Our make out sessions turned into sex with me screaming his name. I should have been embarrassed, but everyone was used to us going at it when I came to see him. Living with him part time made my choice to be his girlfriend a lot easier and I loved to be seen in the papers, on social media, and in his club as his woman. My entire world was consumed by Esteban Munoz, and I wouldn't change anything.

Epilogue: Esteban

Emersyn sat back in the VIP section of *Passions*, my nightclub, holding a book in her hand while the music blasted around the room. All I could do was smile at my baby because nothing about her would ever change and I appreciated that about her personality. Sanya and Raya poured another glass, offering one to her. She didn't bother to look up to see them start dancing in front of the balcony. In the past six months, we'd grown closer, and she'd even decided to move in with me full time and accepted my engagement ring. It was a five carat green emerald set on a silver band. It wrapped around her finger and was the first thing I noticed every morning I woke her. Celebrating her birthday tonight meant I had to accept all of her quirks and she accepted mine. I had a gift to surprise her with and I hoped she would accept it without arguing.

"Esteban, the cake is ready," one of my staff members informed me, standing at the corner of red rope waiting to enter.

Nodding, I waved them in and the bodyguards held

the rope open to set up the cake and candles. The DJ turned the music down and handed the mic to me. I grinned at Emersyn poking her lip out in confusion.

"Baby, stand up." I reached to pull Emersyn into my arms.

Emersyn stood, embarrassed at the spotlight on her. "Esteban, what is going on?"

I kissed the side of her neck. "For your birthday, I wanted to not only surprise you with a party tonight, but to give you something special."

I slipped a hand into my coat pocket, and I took the envelope and handed it to her to open. "Open it, baby."

"Come on, Emersyn!" Sanya shouted as she excitedly sat in Gerald's lap.

Ripping it open, Emersyn's eyes lit up in happiness at what I'd been able to keep to myself.

"When did you have time? I mean we're together every day." Emersyn stretched her arms around my neck. I tugged her close and inhaled her sweet perfume. "The deed to a building?"

I nudged her hair back and caressed her cheek. "I know you love working at the bookstore. Well, this way, you can have your own store."

She nibbled on her top lip. "At first I didn't think I could love you more than the first time you told me you loved me, but seeing this gift means you took time to get to know me." Emersyn sniffled and wiped the tears from her cheeks.

"Nothing is more important than your happiness."

"I hate to leave Louise." Emersyn pouted sadly.

"Louise already knows and even offered to help you get started."

"That's so awesome, Emersyn! Now we can have our

club meetings at a permanent location." Sanya smiled and stood to hug Emersyn, who was staring at the paperwork.

"Time to sing 'Happy Birthday', baby."

"Thank you so much, Esteban. How can I repay you?"

I held her tightly to my chest. "Later when we get home, I can have you all to myself." I sucked on her neck, and she moaned trying to hide her arousal.

"I can't wait."

"Be patient, baby. When I consume you, I will never let you go."

The rest of the party continued with more dancing and drinking. Emersyn let her hair down, pulling me close while rolling her hips and bouncing her curvy ass on my lap. I could already taste her sweet nectar in my mouth.

"Emersyn, stop before I make you mine."

"Too late. I've always been yours." She lifted onto her toes and pressed her lips on top of mine, snaking her tongue inside. I gripped her lower back, pushing her against the wall.

"I'll consume your mind, then your body," I whispered, sliding my hand into her panties.

* * *

I hope you enjoyed Emersyn and Esteban's story, check out another billionaire romance.

"His Peace Her Pleasure" click here https://books2read.com/u/3JJroP a billionaire, steamy romance.

Also steamy romance with that includes bodyguard tropes, one night stands, marriage troubles and more here

"*Seeking In Romance 1-6*" https://books2read.com/u/4ELGLe

Don't forget if you love Fling romances, bodyguard, forced proximity then check out, "**Protecting Chanel**" https://books2read.com/u/mqwPB8

If you love brother's best friend romance, then you'll love "**Sensual**" **here** https://books2read.com/u/49-lYYM with a dash of steamy romance.

Check out Bodyguard Romance, military, romantic suspense here *"Protecting Bria"* https://books2read.com/u/bQJkjd

Follow college romance and more characters in "*Taste*" here https://books2read.com/u/bpz1Ng

How about a steamy, medical romance? Check out **"*Haven*"** https://books2read.com/u/4jAvyZ a steamy enemies to lovers romance.

Please also check out my *"Love Don't Live Here Anymore Vanessa Andrew"* https://books2read.com/u/mBOWGZ a steamy curvy girl, enemies to lovers romance.

Follow that up with a workplace, vacation romance in "**Love Don't Live Here Anymore Isabella Andrew**" https://books2read.com/u/brVNO7

More workplace, boss romances with "**Love by Design Box Set 1-3**" https://books2read.com/u/m2ldEk

Reader Questions

1. Was Esteban right with going behind Emersyn's back to get her phone number?

2. Should Emersyn have played hard to get with Esteban longer?

3. Was Sanya and Raya wrong for leaving Emerson at the coffee shop with Esteban?

4. Did you think Emersyn needed to live life more?

Sneak Peek: Tempt Me

Can Bia finally get over her crush for her brother's best friend turned billionaire businessman?

Kofi stole Bia's heart a long time ago. She's made a habit of ignoring her body whenever he was around. He's a playboy, a billionaire, and completely off limits and now he's her biggest business rival.

Bia's always been his best-friend's little sister, that's why Kofi didn't feel threatened at all when he learned that he and Bia were going to be working together. Besides, he's always waited for the right opportunity to ask her about a text she sent him one drunken night, it's time for her to explain herself.

Stepping into Kofi's world is harder than Bia imagined. Not only is he respected and experienced in his field, but he's also cocky and more handsome than ever before.

Will Kofi get the answers he's looking for, or will Bia bow out before things get too heated in the boardroom?

About the Author

A TENNESSEE NATIVE, and California dreaming Author KeKe Renée is living and striving to continue her passion of writing short story romances in genres ranging from Erotic, Paranormal, and Women's Fiction.

304 Publishing Company

WE SHOWCASE AUTHORS writing Romance, Women's Fiction, Erotic, and Mystery novels. Along with Thriller, Suspense, Poetry, Beauty, and Style Books. Thank you for taking the time out to visit. Join our mailing list to stay updated with new releases and blog posts.

What's Next

Catalog of Releases By Keke Renée

- Wet Heat (Wet Heat Series Book 1)
- Every time We Touch Novelette (Wet Heat Book 2 Series)
- His Peace, Her Pleasure
- Baby, It's Cold Outside
- Love Don't Live Here Anymore, Vanessa Andrew Book 1
- Love Don't Live Here Anymore, Isabella Andrew Book 2
- One Night Only-A Novelette (Love By Design Book 1)
- Cassian and Savannah (Love By Design Book 2)
- Deidra's Love (Love By Design Book 3)
- Protecting Bria (Special Force Operation Alphas)
- Protecting Chanel (Special Force Operation Alphas)
- Haven
- Taste (A New Adult romance)
- Sensual
- Seek To Please
- Seek To Bare

•Seek To Touch
•Seek To Love
•Seek To Trust
•Seek To Earn
•Protecting Yanira (Special Force Operation Alphas)

Thank you so much for reading and if you enjoyed the crazy ride and decide to leave a review we'd truly appreciate the support.

Acknowledgments

I CAN'T MENTION ENOUGH the support and dedication of my author buddies for keeping me uplifted. My behind the scenes team of beta readers, editors, designers, and more. As a writer I continue to strive for the best, and I appreciate each and every one that reads my work. Without your continual feedback I wouldn't be on this path, letting doubts slip away.